This **LONDON** book belongs to:

....

....

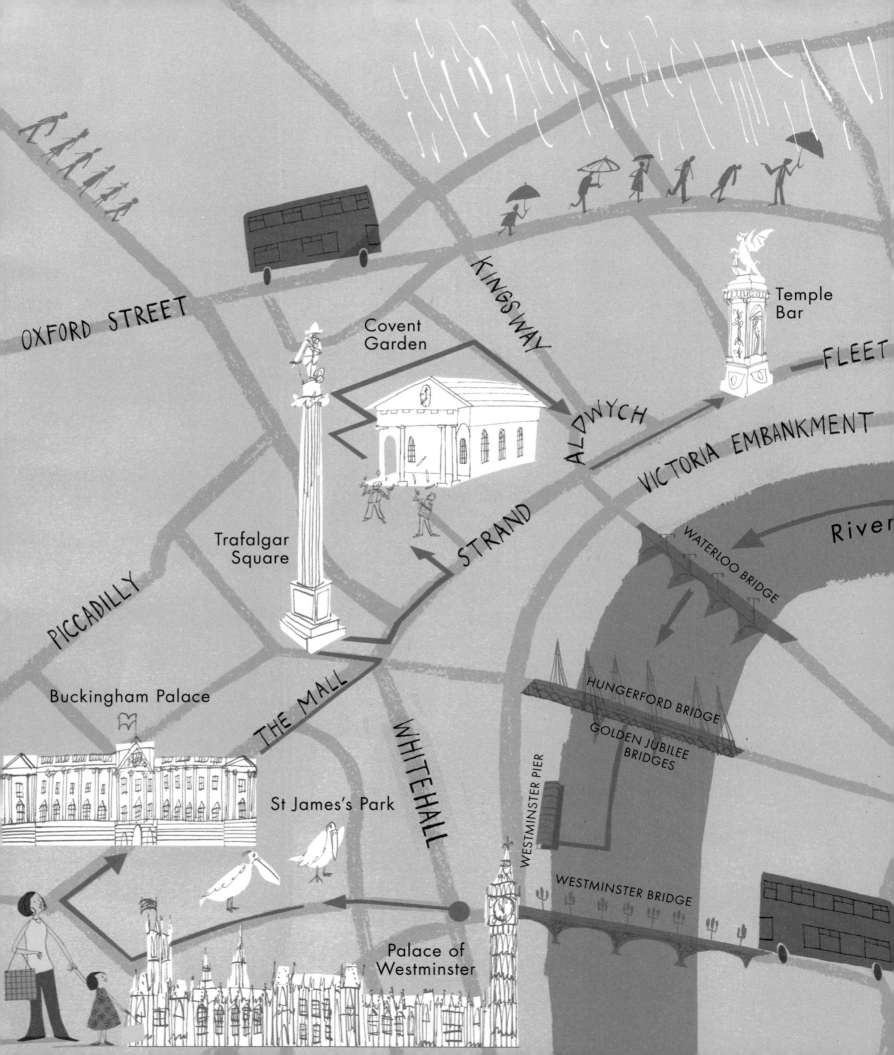

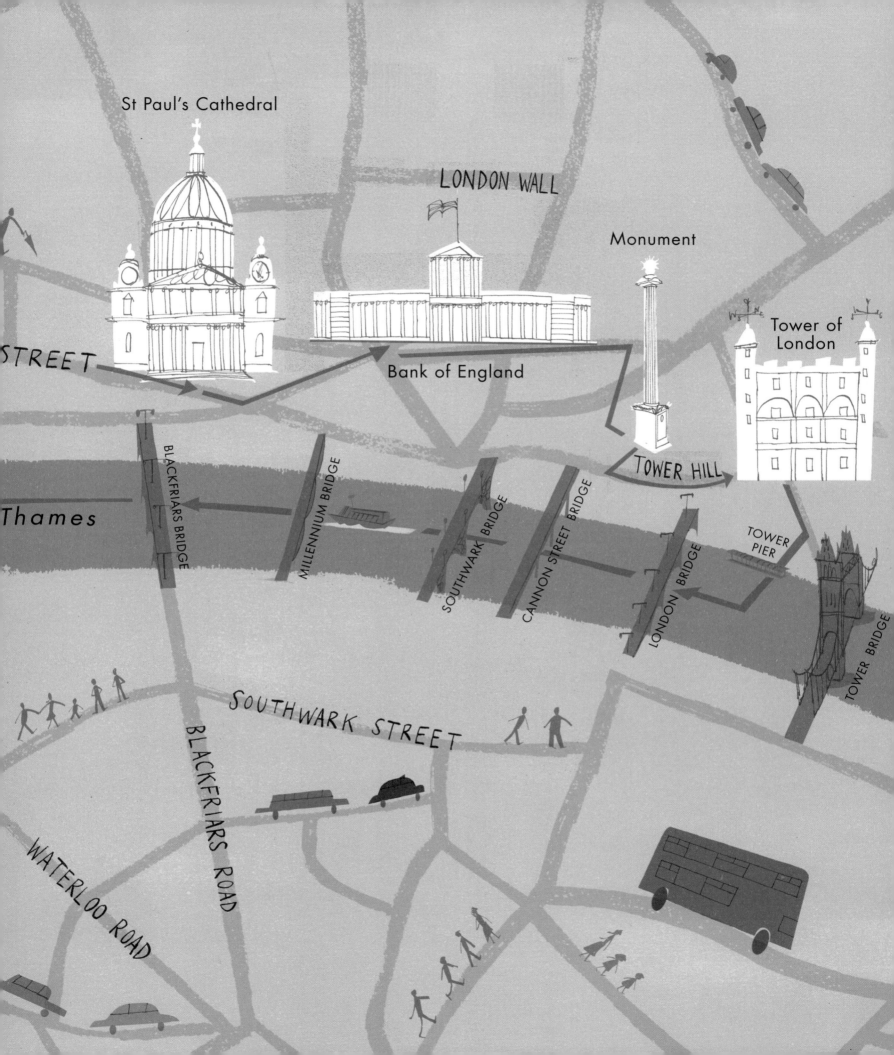

For my beautiful boys,
Billy and Tom

First published 2011 by Walker Books Ltd
87 Vauxhall Walk, London SE11 5HJ

This edition published 2012

4 6 8 10 9 7 5

© 2011 Salvatore Rubbino

The right of Salvatore Rubbino to be identified as author and
illustrator of this work has been asserted by him in accordance
with the Copyright, Designs and Patents Act 1988

This book has been typeset in MKlang Bold and Futura Book

Printed in Belgium

British Library Cataloguing in Publication Data:
a catalogue record for this book is available
from the British Library

ISBN 978-1-4063-3779-2

www.walker.co.uk

WALKER BOOKS
AND SUBSIDIARIES
LONDON · BOSTON · SYDNEY · AUCKLAND

POLICE

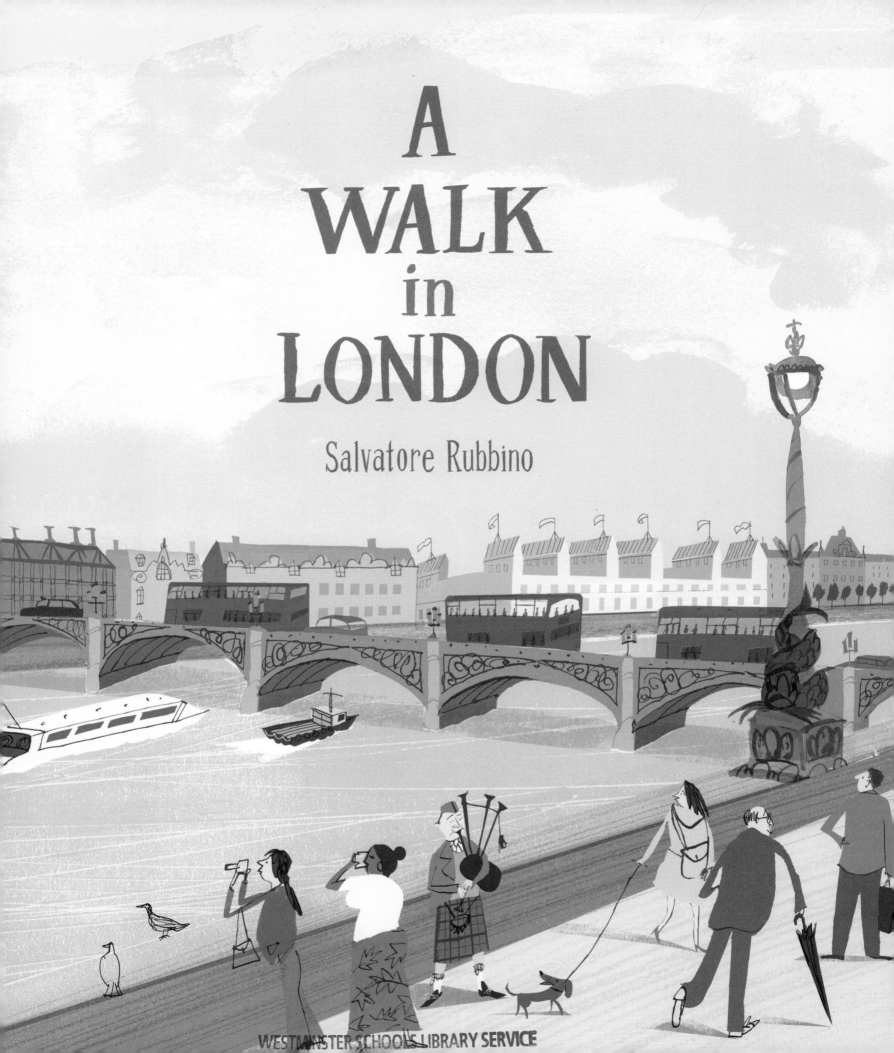

A WALK in LONDON

Salvatore Rubbino

Most people call the clock tower of the Palace of Westminster "Big Ben", but in fact Big Ben is the name of the bell inside the clock.

The clock has been ticking since 1859. It keeps very good time.

London is the capital city of the United Kingdom. It has around 7.5 million citizens.

Double-decker buses have been riding London's streets since the 1930s.

Hello! There's **me**, and that's my mum! We've just got off the bus in Westminster – in the heart of central **London!**

A tall clock strikes. "That's **Big Ben**," Mum tells me. "It's eleven o'clock. Good, we're just in time..."

St James's Park is a "royal" park and lies between three palaces: the Palace of Westminster, Buckingham Palace and St James's Palace.

"In time for what?" I want to know.
"Wait and see!" Mum smiles.
"This way – through **St James's Park**."
The park is full of water,
and the water's full of ducks.
So are the benches...

Over a thousand trees grow in St James's Park.

"Hello!" I say.
"That's a pelican," Mum says.
"It's very rare to meet one."

The first pelicans to live in St James's Park were given to King Charles II in 1664 by the Russian Ambassador.

"Here we are!" Mum says. We've reached the **biggest** house I've ever seen!

"*Buckingham Palace* is where the royal family live," Mum tells me. "Every day, new sentries come to guard it – and there's a ceremony called the Changing of the Guard."

In the yard, a smart black car is waiting. "I think the royal family are going for a drive!" I say.

A flag always flies above the Palace. There are two flags – one for when the monarch's away, and this one for when the monarch's in London.

Buckingham Palace has its own post office, and its own postcode: SW1A 1AA.

Buckingham Palace has 775 rooms, including the Throne Room, the Music Room, the Marble Hall, the Picture Gallery, the Yellow Drawing Room, the Chinese Luncheon Room and the Ballroom.

The Changing of the Guard takes place at 11.30 sharp every morning in spring and summer, and every other morning in autumn and winter.

During the ceremony, the "New Guard" receive the Palace keys from the "Old Guard", while a full military band plays.

Not many people know that London's official central point is on
a roundabout just south of Trafalgar Square.

After the ceremony, Mum takes me to a special place to stand.
"Now you're standing at the very centre
– of the centre –
of London!" she tells me.

We listen to a visitor reading from his guide book:
"From this spot, Manchester is 296 kilometres, Rome is 1,799,
Sydney is 16,898 and the moon is about 386,000..."

"And look, **TRAFALGAR SQUARE** is just
ten metres away!" Mum laughs.

Admiral Nelson died at sea, at the battle of Trafalgar in 1805. This column with his statue at the top stands 51.5 metres high.

Every winter, since 1947, Norway has sent Londoners a very tall Christmas tree. It stands in Trafalgar Square.

Four lions lie round the statue's base to guard it. They are made out of bronze which is kept shiny by all the visitors who come to sit on them.

We cross the traffic and I start to run. There are fountains and some lions I want to sit on!

I'm really hungry! Mum takes me to a café where you can sit outside to eat. We ask for fish and chips.

"This is COVENT GARDEN PIAZZA," Mum says. "No cars allowed!"

Instead the road is full of acrobats and jugglers...

Street entertainers are allowed to perform in Covent Garden every day except Christmas Day.

Not many roads in London are closed to traffic, but Covent Garden Piazza is one of them.

Until 1974, London's biggest fruit-and-flower market was held here every day.

I put some money in the hat of someone standing upside down!

Fish and chips is one of the most popular meals in Britain. About 300 million servings are eaten each year.

London is Europe's third-rainiest city. About 580 millimetres of rain falls here every year.

Oh dear! It's raining! Some people have umbrellas, and some – like us – forgot!

The streets turn shiny. We cross one to a shop that sells exactly what we need!

FOOD & NEWS

29

WE SELL UMBRELLAS

Queen's Head

A London telephone box is a good place to wait out a shower.

West of the dragon, the road is called the Strand and its postcode is W (west) 1.

East of the dragon, it's called Fleet Street and its postcode is E (east) 1.

It's nice and dry under our new umbrella. But "Careful, there's a dragon!" I warn Mum.

"So far we've walked in Westminster," Mum laughs, "but if we step beyond the statue, we'll be in the oldest part of London ...

The emblem of the City is a dragon because in myths, dragons guard treasure and the City is where most of London's banks are.

The City boundary is called Temple Bar.

18

Ye Olde Cheshire Cheese

'the City'. The City's full of history."

It's full of sunshine too!
The rain has gone
away.

The City is
sometimes
called the
Square Mile,
because that's
how big it is.

There has been a cathedral on this site for over 1,400 years.

Next we reach a huge stone church! "We're at **ST PAUL'S CATHEDRAL**," Mum tells me. "Let's go in ...

there's a Whispering Gallery inside."

We climb round
and round

and round,
until we're in the dome.

There are 259 steps up to St Paul's Whispering Gallery.

A whisper against the wall on one side of the dome can be heard 32 metres away on the other.

The Cathedral dome weighs about 64,000 tonnes.

Three St Paul's Cathedrals
have burned to the ground.
This one was designed
by Christopher Wren.

*Mum makes us stand
in different places, then
"Hello?" she whispers – and I jump!
It sounds as if she's right
beside me.*

The streets near the Cathedral have interesting names: Bread Street, Ironmonger Lane – this one's called THREADNEEDLE STREET.

"There's the Bank of England," Mum says. "Britain's oldest bank."

Round the corner, we find the Bank's museum. In the display cases, there's lots of money! Coins ...

Modern British currency has eight coins. They have to be light enough to carry in your pocket, but strong enough to circulate for many years.

British coins used to be made of almost pure silver or gold. Now they are made of less valuable metals, like steel, nickel or brass.

British coins are struck or "minted" at the Royal Mint, which used to be in the Tower of London. Now it's near Cardiff in Wales.

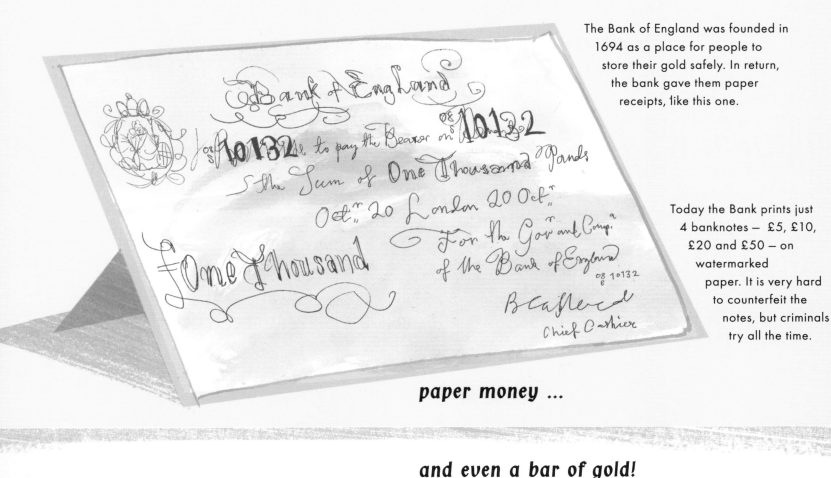

The Bank of England was founded in 1694 as a place for people to store their gold safely. In return, the bank gave them paper receipts, like this one.

Today the Bank prints just 4 banknotes — £5, £10, £20 and £50 — on watermarked paper. It is very hard to counterfeit the notes, but criminals try all the time.

paper money ...

and even a bar of gold!

O O O O O O O F ...

I try to lift it but I'm not strong enough.

Underground, the Bank still stores thousands of bars of 24-carat pure gold in vaults. Each bar is worth over £200,000 and weighs about 13 kilos.

You can climb the 311 spiral steps inside the Monument to see the view from the top. When you come down again, you will be given a certificate!

Christopher Wren designed the Monument to stand 61 metres high because it is 61 metres east of the bakery in Pudding Lane where the Great Fire started.

The column is built out of 800 cubic metres of Portland stone.

We're tired now, so we find a bench and have a sit-down.

Opposite is a tall stone column. "That's called the MONUMENT," Mum says. "It was built in memory of the Great Fire of London, See the bowl of copper flames on top?"

"I like history stories," I tell Mum.
"Then there's one more thing to show you," she says...

The Great Fire of London broke out on 2 September 1666 and lasted for almost five days, burning thousands of City streets and buildings.

The world's first underground trains ran under the river in London. The trains had no windows and passengers found the ride very rough.

UNDERGROUND

MONUMENT STATION

SUNNY SPELLS NEXT WEEK

WOW! A real castle
in the middle of the city!

"Nowadays, kings and queens live
at Buckingham Palace," Mum tells
me, "but long ago they
lived here, at the
TOWER OF LONDON."

JEWE
HOUS

As well as
being a palace,
the Tower was
a prison. Famous
inmates included
Guy Fawkes, Anne
Boleyn and Sir
Walter Raleigh.

We buy tickets and join a guided
tour with a soldier
called a Beefeater!

There are many towers inside the castle walls. The oldest is the White Tower which was built by William the Conqueror in the 1070s.

WHITE TOWER

Seven ravens live at the Tower. The Ravenmaster feeds them 170 grams of raw meat every day, an egg a week and occasionally a rabbit.

BLOODY TOWER

TRAITORS' GATE

The Tower's outer walls are about eight metres high and three metres thick.

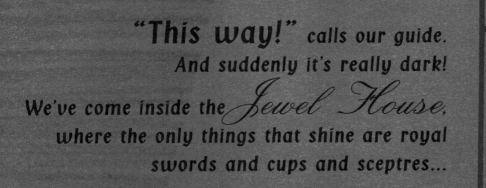

"**This way!**" calls our guide.
And suddenly it's really dark!
We've come inside the *Jewel House*,
where the only things that shine are royal
swords and cups and sceptres...

The Crown Jewels have been kept at the Tower of London since the 14th century.

They have never been stolen, though in 1671, a thief called Thomas Blood tried to take them.

"What makes the crown so sparkly?" I whisper.
"2,868 diamonds!" a boy in our group whispers back.

The Imperial State Crown also has 17 sapphires, 11 emeralds, 5 rubies and 273 pearls in it.

The monarch wears it every year at the State Opening of Parliament.

Until 1749, there was only one way across the Thames in London. Now there are lots, including road bridges, footbridges, rail bridges and tunnels under the riverbed.

More planes fly over London than over any city in the world

More people live in London than in any other city in the EU.

Over 300 different languages are spoken here.

London is about 20 centuries old. The first Romans to settle here came in 43 AD.

The London Eye lifts 3.5 million visitors a year 135 metres high above the city. On a clear day you can see for 40 kilometres in any direction.

The Palace of Westminster is where MPs debate new laws to govern the country. You can visit the public gallery to watch them doing it for free.

The Thames in London is tidal, so its water is partly fresh and partly salt. It is home to lots of fish – including trout, bass and flounder.

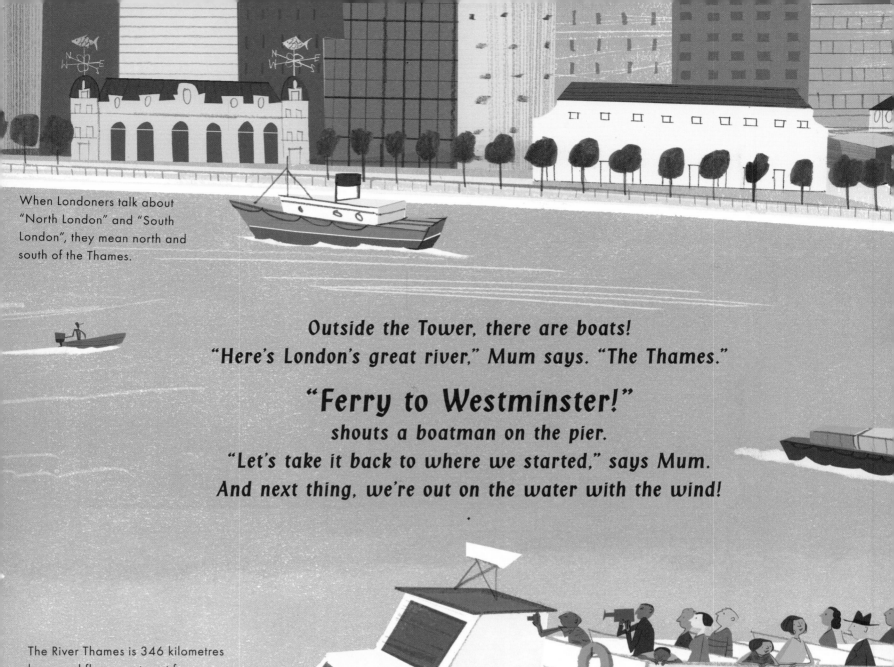

When Londoners talk about "North London" and "South London", they mean north and south of the Thames.

Outside the Tower, there are boats!
"Here's London's great river," Mum says. "The Thames."

"Ferry to Westminster!"
shouts a boatman on the pier.
"Let's take it back to where we started," says Mum.
And next thing, we're out on the water with the wind!

The River Thames is 346 kilometres long, and flows west-east from Gloucestershire to the North Sea.

Altogether, London covers an area of about 1,750 square kilometres. It is divided into 32 districts or "boroughs".

Completed in 1710, St Paul's Cathedral was the city's tallest building for two and a half centuries.

In 1968, the previous London Bridge was sold to an American, who rebuilt it in Arizona.

TATE MODERN, BANKSIDE

SHAKESPEARE'S GLOBE

The word "Th... comes from the... "Tamesa", which... dark or mud...

Back on land, we wait for our bus home.
My legs feel wobbly!

Big Ben strikes.
"Six o'clock,"
Mum counts,
"Just in time," I say.
"For what?" Mum asks.
"To see the royal family!"
I answer, waving
at the smart black car
that's going by...

Although the North Sea is 68 kilometres away, you often see seagulls in London.

Londoners often give new buildings on their skyline nicknames:

this one is known as "the Gherkin". Its real name is 30 St Mary Axe.

Between the 14th and 19th centuries, winters were so cold that the river often froze. Londoners could skate or sledge across it, and "frost fairs" were held on the ice.

...es" ...Celtic ...means ...y.

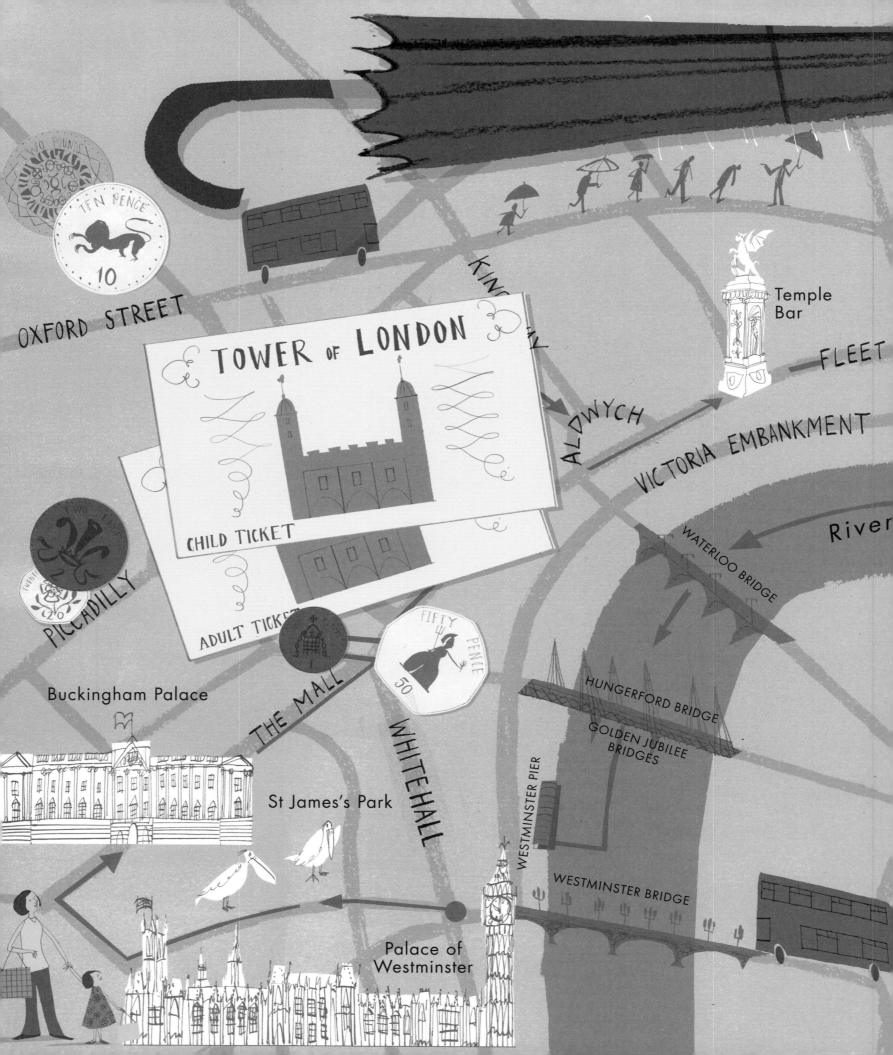

OXFORD STREET

TEN PENCE
10

TWO POUNDS

Temple
Bar

TOWER of LONDON

KINGSWAY

ALDWYCH

FLEET

VICTORIA EMBANKMENT

River

WATERLOO BRIDGE

CHILD TICKET

PICCADILLY

TWENTY
£20

ADULT TICKET

FIFTY PENCE
50

THE MALL

WHITEHALL

HUNGERFORD BRIDGE

GOLDEN JUBILEE
BRIDGES

Buckingham Palace

St James's Park

WESTMINSTER PIER

WESTMINSTER BRIDGE

Palace of
Westminster

St Paul's Cathedral

TREET

hames

BLACKFRIARS BRIDGE

LLENNIUM BRIDGE

BRIDGE

EET BRIDGE

LONDON BRIDGE

Monument

Tower of London

TOWER HILL

TOWER PIER

TOWER BRIDGE

FISH & CHIPS ... £ 10l
MUSHY PEAS ... £ 30u
POT of TEA ... £ cu
CREAM CAKE ... £ 08l

ONE POUND

FIVE PENCE 5

TEN PENCE 1

WATERLOO ROAD

INDEX

Look up the pages to find out
about all these London places:

Did you spot the royal family's car on these pages?
10, 13, 17, 19, 24, 33

Salvatore Rubbino loves walking about in cities.
He always checks the weather forecast before he sets out.
"If it looks like rain," he says, "I take my umbrella – there's
nothing worse than trying to draw on soggy paper!"

If you enjoyed this book, why not take a walk around another city!

ISBN 978-1-4063-2180-7

Available from all good booksellers

www.walker.co.uk